The Special Delivery

Illustrated by Richard Courtney

Random House 🏠 New York

A Random House PICTUREBACK® Book

Thomas the Tank Engine & Friends

A BRITT ALLCROFT COMPANY PRODUCTION

Based on The Railway Series by The Rev W Awdry.

Copyright © Gullane (Thomas) LLC 2002. All rights reserved under International and Pan-American Copyright Conventions.
Published in the United States by Random House Children's Books, a division of Random House, Inc., New York, and
simultaneously in Canada by Random House of Canada Limited, Toronto.

www.randomhouse.com/kids www.thomasthetankengine.com

Library of Congress Cataloging-in-Publication Data

Awdry, W. The special delivery / illustrated by Richard Courtney. p. cm. — (A Random House pictureback book)
"Based on the Railway series by W. Awdry." — T.p. verso. SUMMARY: Thomas, Gordon, and the other trains try to deliver
an urgent package to Sir Topham Hatt as quickly as possible.

ISBN 0-375-81494-9 [1. Railroads—Trains—Fiction. 2. Hats—Fiction.] I. Courtney, Richard, 1955– ill. Awdry, W. Railway series.
III. Random House pictureback. PZ7.S74117 2002 [E]—dc21 2001019695

Printed in the United States of America First Edition 25 24 23 22 21

Cranky was unloading a box for Sir Topham Hatt. The box was marked URGENT.

"Humpf," creaked Cranky. "What's so *urgent* about this package?"

Thomas heard Cranky's question.

"If it says *urgent,* we should get it to Sir Topham Hatt as fast as we can!" he said. "I'll take it!"

Just then, Gordon pulled up next to Thomas.

"An *urgent* package needs a speedy train," said Gordon. "I'm the fastest train here, so *I* will have to take the package."

Gordon took the package and set off immediately.

Thomas was left behind. "*I* could have gotten it there quickly," he peeped.

Gordon hurried down the track and took a hilly shortcut. Suddenly, he saw a red signal. Some rocks had fallen across his path. He was stuck!

Just then, Toby came by on an open track.

"Help!" said Gordon. "I have an *urgent* package for Sir Topham Hatt."

"I can take it down the hill," said Toby.

"Thank you!" Gordon called as Toby chugged away.

Toby clickety-clacked quickly down the hill.

Percy was waiting at the bottom.
"Thank you for bringing the *urgent* package down," said
Percy. "Now I can take it to Sir Topham Hatt."

"Sir Topham Hatt will be very proud of me," Percy
tooted as he hurried along.

Percy rounded a bend and saw James ahead of him pulling two Troublesome Trucks. James was going very slowly because the trucks had their brakes on.

"*We* want to take the package," said the Troublesome Trucks. "We won't release our brakes until you give it to us."

Percy was very mad, but he knew that the *urgent* package had to get to Sir Topham Hatt quickly. With a sigh, he gave it to the trucks.

"No more trouble from you trucks," said James. The trucks released their brakes. James and the trucks quickly left Percy behind.

James was glad that he would be the one to deliver this *urgent* package now.

James was going so fast he almost didn't see . . .

. . . the broken track!

"Oh, no!" wailed James. "Now Sir Topham Hatt will never get his *urgent* package."

"I'll take the *urgent* package," said Harold, landing next to James. He took the package and flew off.

Harold soared over the countryside. He looked down and
saw Thomas pulling into Tidmouth Station.
    Thomas had been faster than Gordon after all!

"Where's my package?" Sir Topham Hatt asked.

Just then, Harold landed. "I have it, sir," he said. Then he told Thomas and Sir Topham Hatt what had happened.

Finally, Sir Topham Hatt opened the *urgent* package.
What could be inside?

It's a shiny new hat!

"Just in time for tonight's big party," Sir Topham Hatt said, putting the hat on his head. "And, Thomas, next time there is an *urgent* package . . ."

"... I want *you* to bring it!"